Sleepover Squad

GIRLS AGAINST BOYS

P. J. DENTON

SLEEPOVER SQUAD

GiRLS AGAiNST BOYS

Illustrated by Julia Denos

SCHOLASTIC INC.

ISBN 978-0-545-55936-2

12 11 10 9 8 7 6 5 4 3 2 1   13 14 15 16 17 18/0

Printed in the U.S.A.   40

First Scholastic printing, May 2013

Designed by Karin Paprocki
The text of this book was set in Cochin.

1

A Kitten Named Mittens

"Oh my gosh!" Kara Wyatt rolled over on her back on the grass and giggled as a tiny black-and-white kitten crawled up her shoulder. "Taylor, Mittens is soooo cute!"

Taylor Kent laughed as her new kitten batted a tiny white paw at Kara's wavy red hair. "I know," she said. "I can't believe my parents actually let me get her!"

"Be careful," Emily McDougal warned as

Mittens jumped down and sniffed at a dandelion in the grass. "Don't let her wander too far. We don't want her to get lost outside."

Jo Sanchez reached over to pet Mittens. "Don't worry, Em. I don't think she can run very fast on her tiny little legs. Besides, how far could she wander with all four of us staring at her?" She giggled, then sighed. "I guess I'm the only member of the Sleepover Squad without a pet now."

Taylor, Jo, Emily, and Kara had formed a club called the Sleepover Squad. They took turns hosting sleepovers at each of their houses as often as they could.

But today the girls weren't having a sleepover. They had all gathered in Taylor's backyard to play with her new kitten. Mittens had only been a member of the Kent family for a little over a day. Taylor had always wanted to have a pet, but up until now her parents had always said no.

She'd had to settle for playing with Kara's dog, Chester, or Emily's cat, Mi-Mo.

But now Taylor's parents had finally decided she was responsible enough to help take care of a pet. They had taken Taylor to the animal shelter, where she had picked out Mittens. Mittens was going to be an indoor cat, but it was such a nice spring day that the girls had decided to take her outside for a while to play in the Kents' square, grassy backyard.

Taylor reached over and tickled Mittens under the chin. The kitten started to purr loudly. Just then there was a sudden loud shout from the yard next door. Mittens jumped and stopped purring, her eyes wide and her nose twitching.

"Who was that?" Kara asked in surprise, looking over toward the next yard to see who had made the noise.

Taylor made a face. She and her parents lived in town, which meant the houses were fairly close together. Normally, she liked being close to their neighbors on each side. But over the past few days, that had changed — at least when it came to one particular neighbor.

"Ugh." She picked up Mittens to let the kitten know she shouldn't be scared. "I forgot to tell you guys. That's Stan."

"Who?" Emily looked confused. "I thought Mr. and Mrs. Sampson lived over there. Is

Stan their grandson or something?"

Taylor shook her head. "The Sampsons moved out a couple of weeks ago," she explained. "They went to live in Florida. The new owners are the Martins. They have a son named Stan who's our age."

"Really? That's cool." Jo tucked her dark hair behind her ear and shrugged. "You always complain about how there's no one our age on this block."

"No, it's *not* cool," Taylor corrected with a shudder. "Stan's family only moved in this past Friday. But I can already tell that he's totally obnoxious!"

Just then a boy came into view beyond the tidy hedge that separated the two yards. He was about Taylor's height, with messy brown hair and round cheeks.

Taylor wished they'd decided to stay inside to play with Mittens. But it was too late now. Stan spotted them right away.

"Hi, Taylor," he said, pushing his way through the hedge and wandering toward them. "Hey, what are you doing hanging out with a bunch of girls? With a name like Taylor, I thought you were a boy."

Taylor rolled her eyes. "Very funny," she said. Mittens was wriggling, so she set her down on the grass. "It's almost as funny as it was the first ten times you said it."

Kara giggled. "Good one, Taylor."

Stan stared at Kara and grinned. "Whoa,"

he said. "You must eat a ton of carrots."

Emily furrowed her brow, looking confused. "What do you mean?" she asked. "How can you tell what she eats?"

"Just look at her hair!" Stan pointed at Kara's head. "How else would it end up bright orange like that? What's your name—Carrotina?"

"Just ignore him, Kara," Jo advised.

"Kara?" Stan let out a shout of laughter. "Are you serious? Your name's really Kara? That totally sounds like it's short for Carrotina. I knew it! Kara Carrotina, Kara Carrotina!"

Kara sighed. "Great," she muttered. "Just what we need. Another obnoxious boy around here."

Taylor knew that Kara was thinking about her four brothers. She always said they were the most obnoxious boys in the world. But Taylor was already convinced that Stan could give them a run for their money.

She was about to come to Kara's defense by calling Stan a name in return—like Stanley Stupidhead. But she remembered just in time that her parents had asked her to be nice to the new neighbors. So she bit her tongue.

"Come on," she said to her friends instead. "Maybe we should play with Mittens inside for a while."

"Girls!" Gloria, the Kents' housekeeper, stuck her head out the back door. "Bring the kitten back into the house, please. Emily's father is here to drive her and Jo home. And Kara, your mother just called and said it's time to head home for dinner."

"Coming, Gloria," Taylor called. Both her parents worked long hours at their jobs, and Gloria watched Taylor whenever they weren't home. Sometimes she also came for a little while on the weekend, especially if Mr. and Mrs. Kent had errands to run or work to do at home. She had been doing all that for as long as Taylor could remember.

Gloria lived in her own house on the other side of town, but other than that she was just like a member of the family.

"Aw, I wish we didn't have to go." Emily scooped up Mittens and gave her a gentle hug. The kitten batted at her long pale-blond hair, which made Emily giggle. "I could stay here and play with Mittens all night!"

"Hey, that's an awesome idea, Emmers!" Taylor exclaimed. "Isn't it time for another sleepover?"

Jo smiled. "Definitely. We haven't had one in . . ." She paused for a few seconds. "Um, I think it's been twenty-two days."

Taylor grinned. That was just like Jo—she liked to be exact about things.

"Twenty-two days is way too long," Kara said.

"Totally," Taylor agreed. "I'll ask my parents if I can have our next sleepover here on Saturday night. We can make it all about kittens!"

"A kitten sleepover?" Stan put in with a snort. "Sounds awfully girly for someone with a boy's name. Plus, who ever heard of a giant walking carrot going to a sleepover?"

Taylor rolled her eyes. She had almost forgotten he was still standing there.

"Come on, girls," she said, already heading toward the house. "Let's go inside. We can finish talking about the sleepover in there."

2

Birds of a Feather

Taylor stepped out onto her front porch and took a deep breath of fresh morning air. She loved springtime. Everything seemed bright and warm and clear after the cold winter. Birds were chirping in the trees, and tons of daffodils were blooming in yards up and down the tree-lined street.

But she wasn't really thinking about any of that as she headed down the steps to the front walk. The evening before, after her friends had left, she'd asked her parents about the sleepover. They'd said yes right away.

Taylor wasn't a very patient person. It was hard for her to wait for things, even though the sleepover was less than a week away. To distract herself from being impatient, she had done exactly what Jo would have done. She'd started making plans. After finishing her dinner and her homework, she'd sat down at her desk and written out a whole list of ideas for the sleepover.

It didn't look much like one of Jo's lists. Jo was very organized. Everything she did was neat and tidy. Her lists were usually divided into categories and columns.

Taylor's list wasn't organized at all. She'd just scribbled down all her ideas as she thought of them. There were doodles of Mittens in the corners of the page.

Still, she knew she had some great ideas for the party. One was to play games in the backyard, like soccer and badminton. Taylor loved all sports, especially soccer.

But she knew her friends weren't as crazy about sports as she was. So she'd also come up with some ideas she thought they would like. She was excited to tell them all about her plans, especially since she knew they would probably come up with even more good plans. Everyone always said that Emily was creative—that meant she was good at coming up with ideas. And Kara loved to have fun. She was sure to have some ideas as well. Taylor would get to tell her about the sleepover first, since Kara lived only a few blocks away and the two of them always walked to school together.

When she reached the sidewalk, Taylor turned right. She was thinking so hard about the sleepover that she almost didn't hear someone calling her name. But finally she heard it. She blinked and looked around. Stan's mother was standing on the porch of her house. She was dressed in jeans and holding a lamp and a paper bag. Her blond hair was in a ponytail. Taylor guessed that she was still unpacking from moving in.

"Hi, Mrs. Martin." Taylor walked over and stopped at the bottom of the porch steps. Even though Stan was obnoxious, his parents both seemed normal. In fact, Mrs. Martin seemed really nice.

"Good morning, Taylor," Mrs. Martin said. "I'm so glad I caught you. I wonder if you could do me a favor?"

"Sure, Mrs. M. What is it?" Taylor said politely.

Mrs. Martin smiled. "Could you show Stan how to get to school?" she asked. "It's his first day, and I'd planned to walk him there myself, but the plumber is due any minute so I really can't leave." She shrugged. "Besides, I'm sure he'd much rather walk with you."

Taylor wasn't so sure about that. She

was sure that she definitely didn't want to walk with *him*. But she knew it wouldn't be polite to say that to Stan's mother. She was trapped!

"No problem," she said weakly. She already knew that Stan was her age. But she realized she hadn't really thought about what that meant, like that he would be in her grade at school. Just what the third grade needed—another obnoxious boy!

Just then Stan popped out the front door. "Hey, Mom, where's my lunch?" he exclaimed.

"Right here, dear." Mrs. Martin handed him the paper bag she was holding. "Are you ready to go? Taylor just graciously offered to walk you to school. Isn't that nice?"

Stan grinned. "Yeah. Thanks, Taylor. You're the best next-door neighbor ever."

"Come on," Taylor said. She guessed that he was just being polite in front of his mom. Kara's brothers did the same thing.

"We'd better get going. You don't want to be late on your first day, do you?"

Taylor's guess was right. As soon as Stan's mother said good-bye and went back in the house, he stopped being polite.

"Hey, Taylor," he said as they walked down the sidewalk. "Will you show me the boys' bathroom when we get to school? Oops! I forgot—you're not a boy. At least, that's what you keep saying. I still don't believe it."

Taylor gritted her teeth. She still remembered what her parents had told her. *Be polite,* she told herself now. *All you have to do is survive Stan's stupid teasing until you get to school. Then you can ditch him.*

When they reached the corner, she said hello to the crossing guard. There were no cars coming, so the guard waved them across right away.

"Hurry up," Taylor told Stan as they

headed across. "We have to stop and pick up Kara."

"You mean Carrotina?" Stan laughed at his own joke. "Cool. I forgot to ask her yesterday if she eats a lot of oranges, too."

Most mornings, Taylor had to wait for Kara to finish getting ready. She was always running late. She said it was because she had to share a bathroom with all four of her brothers.

But today Kara was waiting in front of her house. She frowned when she spotted Stan.

"What's *he* doing here?" she asked Taylor.

"Aw, aren't you glad to see me, Carrotina?" Stan said with a grin. "I'm so insulted!"

"Just ignore him," Taylor advised. "Listen, I had some cool ideas for our kitten sleepover. What if we borrow some of my mom's makeup to draw cat whiskers on our faces?"

Kara looked excited. "Ooh, that sounds fun!"

"Meow!" Stan said. "Your kitten sleep-over sounds pretty boring so far. If you guys are going to have a sleepover, you should at least make it about something cool, like race cars or outer space."

"In case you didn't notice, nobody asked you," Kara told him.

Stan gasped loudly. "Oh my gosh!" he yelled, pointing at Kara. "I can't believe it. It's a talking carrot!"

A few older kids were walking ahead of them. Several heard Stan and looked back curiously. Two or three girls giggled.

Taylor clenched her fists at her side. "Listen, Stan," she began.

"Don't answer him," Kara said quickly. "He's just looking for attention, like my stupid brothers. Maybe if we ignore him, he'll shut up."

Taylor followed Kara's advice. But it didn't

work. Stan kept teasing them all the way to school. Taylor thought they'd never get there.

But finally they arrived. Principal Lewis was standing in the lobby, as usual. She walked over when she saw Taylor, Kara, and Stan come in.

"Good morning, girls. And hello there, you must be Stanley," the principal said with a smile. "Your mother called and said you were on your way. Welcome to Oak Tree Elementary! Now come with me and we'll get you all settled in."

"Whew!" Taylor said as the principal disappeared into her office with Stan. "That's a relief."

"I hope he's not in our class," Kara said. "We have enough dumb boys as it is."

Taylor nodded. There were two third-grade classes at Oak Tree Elementary. The Sleepover Squad was in one, and if they were lucky, Stan would be in the other one!

But it turned out they *weren't* lucky. Attendance had barely started when the door opened and Principal Lewis walked in. Stan was right behind her.

"Kids, I'd like to introduce your new classmate," the principal announced. "This is Stanley Martin."

"Hi, everybody," Stan said with a wave.

"Cool!" Max Wolfe called out from his seat in the back. "We need another boy in this class."

"Yeah!" his friend Randy Blevins shouted. He loved to shout. "Come sit by us, Stanley!"

"Okay. You can call me Stan," Stan said as he hurried toward them.

"Uh-oh," Jo said. "Looks like Max and Randy have a new friend."

Kara rolled her eyes. "Oh, great," she muttered. "Now the terrible two will be the terrible three."

Taylor knew what she meant. Randy and Max were the most obnoxious boys in the third grade.

Just then there was a loud burst of laughter. When Taylor looked back, all three boys were staring at Kara. Taylor was pretty sure she heard one of them say something about carrots.

"I guess what my mom says is true," Emily said. "Birds of a feather flock together."

"Yeah," Taylor said with a groan. "Especially stupid, loud, obnoxious birds!"

3

Copycats

"It was so cute," Taylor said as she picked up her sandwich. "Remember how I was telling you that Mittens likes to play with my shoelaces when I tie my sneakers? Well, I forgot to say that she also likes to play with my pencil when I write. Last night I couldn't finish my spelling homework until she fell asleep!"

Kara giggled. "Mittens is so adorable!"

"I know," Jo agreed, reaching for her

milk. "I can't wait until the sleepover."

Emily nodded. "We'll be able to play with Mittens all night!"

It was Wednesday, and the four friends were in the school lunchroom. The sleepover was only three days away now, and Taylor couldn't wait. She and her friends had all sorts of great activities planned. But not *too* many. They wanted to spend most of their time with Mittens!

"I helped my dad get out the badminton set last night," she said. "Maybe you guys can come over on Friday after school and help set it up."

"I'll come," Kara said.

Emily looked disappointed. "I can't," she reminded Taylor. "I have my riding lesson on Friday."

"And I have my tennis lesson," Jo added. "Sorry."

Taylor shrugged. In all the excitement of planning the party, she'd forgotten about her friends' lessons. "That's okay," she said. "As long as Kara comes over to help me, I'm sure we can—"

"Hey! Guess what?" Stan yelled, running up to their table and interrupting.

Kara frowned at him. "Do you mind? We're trying to have a conversation here."

Taylor nodded. She was so busy with her sleepover plans that she'd almost forgotten about her new neighbor. Luckily, Randy and Max both walked to school too. So Stan walked with them now.

"Guess what?" Stan said again. By now Max and Randy were there, too. All three boys were grinning.

"What?" Emily asked. She was nice to everyone—even boys.

"We just thought you might like to know," Max said. "We're having a sleepover at Stan's house. It's this Saturday night."

"What?" Kara blurted out, her hazel eyes going wide with surprise. "But we're having a sleepover at Taylor's this Saturday!"

"Really?" Randy raised his eyebrows so

high they disappeared beneath his shaggy bangs. "Oh my goodness gracious!"

Stan slapped his cheeks and gasped loudly. "I can't believe it!"

"Me neither!" Max cried.

Jo rolled her eyes. "Don't pay any attention to them," she advised the other girls. "They're just goofing off because they heard about our sleepover."

"Yeah." Kara frowned. "You guys aren't really having a sleepover. So stop pretending you are."

Stan smirked. "You're wrong, Carrotina," he said. "We *are* having a sleepover at my house. You can call my parents and ask them if you don't believe me."

Taylor narrowed her eyes and stared at him. He didn't look like he was lying. "Are you serious?" she blurted out angrily. "You guys are such . . . such . . . such copycats!"

Emily looked worried. She didn't like it when anyone fought or got angry. "It's okay, Taylor," she said. "It's no big deal."

"It's *not* okay. Stan is only having a sleepover because he wants to bug me!" Taylor exclaimed.

"Why are you two so excited about it, anyway?" Jo pointed at Randy and Max. "You guys only met Stan on Monday."

"Yeah," Kara said. "It's not like you're lifelong best friends like the Sleepover Squad. Anyway, sleepovers are for girls!"

"Nuh-uh," Max said. "Anything girls can do, boys can do better."

"And cooler," Stan added.

Randy grinned. "And awesomer!"

"'Awesomer' isn't even a word," Jo said.

Randy shrugged. "It is now," he said. "Our party is going to be way awesomer than any pathetic girl party!"

"Whatever," Kara muttered. "Who cares what they think, anyway?"

Jo nodded. "Let them have their stupid party. We all know ours will be more fun."

But Taylor wasn't ready to let the boys get away with thinking they could throw a better sleepover than the girls could. Everyone knew the Sleepover Squad's parties were the best!

"You guys are dreaming," she said. "Our sleepover will be a million times better than yours. No, make that a *trillion* times better!"

"Oh yeah?" Stan smirked. "Well, maybe we should make you prove it!"

Max snorted with laughter and elbowed Randy in the side. Then all three boys started laughing and ran away.

Taylor glared after them. "What was that supposed to mean?" she muttered.

Jo shrugged. "Who cares?" she said, picking up her juice box.

Emily nodded. She just looked relieved that the boys were gone.

But Kara bit her lip, looking worried. "I hope they're not planning something."

"What do you mean?" Jo asked.

"What if they try to mess up our sleep-over?" Kara said. "They might try to sabotage us by playing practical jokes or spying on us or something."

Taylor felt a twinge of concern. After all, Kara was the expert on obnoxious boy behavior. Her brothers always tried to mess up their sleepovers when they were at Kara's house.

But she shrugged off her worry quickly. "Just let them try," she said. "If your brothers can't get the best of us, Kara, those three nerds don't have a chance."

Emily giggled. "True," she said. "Kara's brothers are master troublemakers."

"Yeah," Jo agreed. "Anyway, there's no sense worrying about it. All we can do is wait and see what happens."

4

A Sleepover Challenge

"How's this?" Kara called from the far side of the yard.

Taylor looked up from dragging her family's badminton set across the grass and squinted at her. The afternoon sun was shining brightly. It was Friday afternoon, and the weather was supposed to be just as nice the next day. Taylor was glad about that. It meant they could spend lots of time outside during the sleepover.

Maybe they could even bring Mittens out to play on the lawn again for a little while.

Kara was standing by a bunch of empty wastebaskets, which she had just finished setting up in a sort of triangle. There were three wastebaskets at the front, then two behind that, and one at the very back. They would be the goals for a beanbag-toss game Taylor had invented. Now that the sleepover was only a day away, she was more excited than ever. Just as she'd planned, there would be lots of activities that everyone would enjoy.

Taylor knew she would have tons of fun running around outside in the yard. Jo would be happy that they were play-ing badminton, since it was a lot like her favorite sport, tennis. Emily had promised to bring over some of her father's delicious homemade sugar-cookie dough. The girls were going to make cat-shaped cookies and decorate them. They would all have fun doing that, especially Emily. Taylor had also brought down the costume box from the attic and borrowed some of her mom's old shoes and jewelry so they could play dress-up. Kara would definitely love that. And of course all four of them would enjoy playing with Mittens!

"That looks perfect, K," she called. "We can draw the throw line right there by the rosebush. Now come help me set up the badminton net. I can never get it straight by myself."

"Okay." Kara brushed off her hands and hurried toward her. "Did Em's dad drop off their croquet set?"

"Uh-huh. It's in the house."

"Cool." Kara giggled. "I just hope I'm better at croquet this time. When we played before at Em's sleepover, I kept hitting my foot instead of the ball, remember?"

Taylor grinned. She did remember that. Before she could say so, a new voice broke in: "Yeah, that's why girls shouldn't even try to play sports. Everyone knows they're only good at tea parties and putting on dresses."

Taylor whirled around so fast that she almost dropped the badminton net. Stan was grinning at them from the other side of the hedge. His two new friends Max and Randy were with him.

"Do you mind?" she snapped. "This is private property, you know."

"Why are you even bothering to set up all that sports stuff?" Randy spoke up. "Shouldn't you be inside, drawing pictures of kittycats or something?"

Max laughed. "Yeah," he said. "Or maybe they're going to make that kitten play sports, and they'll all dress up like cheerleaders with pom-poms."

"Just ignore them, Taylor," Kara said with a sniff. "They're just trying to make us mad."

Taylor knew she was right. Then again,

she'd been doing her best to ignore them all week. And so far it wasn't doing much good. She took a deep breath and started unfolding the badminton net. Maybe the boys would take the hint and go away.

"Hey, Taylor," Randy said. "Are you planning to wear that net as some kind of girly-girl dress?"

Stan laughed so hard that he snorted. "That has to be it. What else would a

bunch of girly-girls be doing with some-thing like that?"

That was too much for Taylor. "Oh yeah?" she yelled, jabbing the post of the net into the ground so hard she almost bent it. "If you boys are so great at sports, why don't you come over here right now and see if you can beat me at badminton? I'll show you that girls can play sports!"

Max laughed. "Yeah, right."

Taylor folded her arms over her chest. "What, are you scared? You know I'll beat you, right?"

"No way," Randy answered immedi-ately. "I can beat you at anything, anytime, anywhere."

Taylor bent down and picked up two badminton rackets. "Oh yeah? Then prove it."

"I have a better idea." Stan spoke up before Randy could respond. "A sleepover challenge!"

"Huh?" Taylor blinked, confused. "What are you talking about?"

Stan grinned. "A sleepover challenge," he repeated. "All of you against all of us, tomorrow during our sleepovers."

Taylor stopped to think about that. She was pretty good at badminton, and Jo was even better. "Sure, you're on," she said. "But you'd better prepare yourselves. We're totally going to cream you at badminton."

"I'm not just talking about badminton," Stan said with a sly grin. "I'm talking about a real sleepover challenge. We can beat you girls at any of your silly little games you want to name, like badminton or whatever. But you also have to compete against us in anything *we* name too."

"That's right," Max put in, looking interested. "*Anything.*"

Kara made a face. "Don't be stupid," she said. "Why would we want to waste our time on that? Unlike you, we have better stuff to do at our sleepovers."

Stan shrugged. "Fine," he said. "If you're too wimpy and girly and scared to do anything except pat little kittens . . ."

Taylor felt her heart start to pump faster, just like it always did at the start of a big soccer game. She'd never backed down from a challenge in her life, and she wasn't about to start now.

"No way, we're not scared of you," she said. "You're on!"

5

A Different Kind of Sleepover

"Awesome!" Stan grinned. "See you girls tomorrow!"

"Yeah," Randy said. "Get ready to lose!"

Max just laughed. All three of the boys turned and ran off into Stan's house.

As soon as they were gone, Kara whirled to face Taylor. She looked horrified.

"Are you crazy?" she cried. "Why did you agree to their stupid challenge idea? It's going to ruin the whole sleepover!"

Taylor shrugged. "No, it won't. It will be fun to beat them."

"Fun?" Kara shuddered. "No way. It sounds too much like staying home and dealing with my brothers."

"Oh, come on. This is no big deal. Once we beat them at a few things, those boys will probably give up." Taylor smiled just thinking about that. She could already picture the look on Stan's face when the girls beat the boys at badminton. And croquet. And everything else. Taylor loved winning, but it would be even better winning against three boys who thought girls couldn't play sports. In fact, she could hardly wait!

Kara still looked doubtful. "Maybe we should stay inside tomorrow when the sleepover starts," she suggested. "If we just ignore the boys for a while, they'll probably get distracted playing ninjas or something and forget all about their stupid challenge."

It was pretty clear that Kara wasn't very excited about the sleepover challenge. Then again, Kara was always a little suspicious of new things. Especially new things that might involve getting dirty or running around a lot. Still, Taylor figured Kara would change her mind once she saw how much fun it was to win against the boys.

"Come on," she said, dropping the badminton rackets on the grass and heading for the back door. "Let's see if Jo-Jo and Emmers are home yet. I want to tell them about the challenge."

Soon she was on the phone, telling Jo what had happened. "A sleepover challenge?" Jo said. She didn't sound much more excited than Kara had. "I thought we were going to spend most of our time tomorrow playing with Mittens. This challenge thing sounds kind of boring."

"No way. It'll be fun, I promise," Taylor said. "We'll be doing all the stuff we

planned anyway, only it's going to be even better because we'll be making Randy and Max and Stan eat their words at the same time."

"I thought you were mad about the boys having a sleepover on the same night as ours," Jo said. "Now you've practically invited them to *our* sleepover. That doesn't make much sense."

Taylor laughed. "Maybe not, but I never said I was as logical as you, Jo-Jo!" she teased cheerfully. "Anyway, it'll be great, you'll see. I've got to go now—I need to call Emmers next."

Emily sounded even less thrilled about the sleepover challenge than Jo and Kara had. "Um, maybe I'll just watch you guys," she said uncertainly. "You know I always get kind of nervous doing stuff like that."

Taylor had forgotten about that, but now she remembered. Emily was always happy to come and cheer her on at her soccer games, but she didn't usually like playing sports herself. Even in gym class or at field day at school, she sometimes got so nervous that she forgot stuff like which way she was supposed to run.

"Don't worry, this is different," Taylor said into the phone. "It's not like being on a soccer team or anything. It's more like playing croquet and other games with your friends at a sleepover. You like doing that, right?"

"Yes," Emily said softly.

"There you go," Taylor said, feeling proud of herself. Now she was being almost as logical as Jo! "The only difference is, we'll be trying to beat those boys at the same time. That will make it even more fun!"

Just then Gloria came into the room to tell them that Kara's older brother had arrived to pick her up. Taylor said good-bye to Emily, then walked Kara to the door.

"See you tomorrow for the sleepover," Taylor said.

Kara glanced out the door. Her brother Chip was out in Taylor's yard, playing with his Hacky Sack. "Hey, Taylor, are you sure you don't want to invite all my brothers to the sleepover too, while you're at it?" she said, rolling her eyes.

Taylor grinned. "That's a good idea!" she joked. "Hey, Chip!"

Kara let out a squeak of horror. She dashed out the front door and slammed it

behind her before Taylor could say anything else.

Taylor laughed. She could tell that Kara
still wasn't very excited about the sleepover
challenge. But she wasn't too worried. She
was sure that all her friends would step
up to the plate when the time came. After
all, they couldn't let a bunch of boys beat
them, could they?

That night after dinner, she brought
Mittens up to her room. Then she sat down
at her desk and pulled out a clean sheet of
paper. She wanted to think of some really
good challenges for the next day—ones the
girls would be certain to win.

She picked up a pencil and wrote down
badminton and *croquet*. She was sure they
could win at both of those. After that she
chewed on the eraser, trying to think of
more.

"Ow!" she blurted out as she felt a prick
on her ankle.

Looking down, she saw that Mittens was pawing at her. Her sharp little claws had gone right through Taylor's socks. She smiled and reached down to scratch the kitten under her chin.

"Aw, you want to play, don't you?" she said.

She wished she could stop and play with the kitten. But she didn't have time. She was sure the boys were next door, plotting all kinds of ridiculous challenges of their own, and she wanted to be ready.

Glancing around the room, she spotted an old shoelace lying on the rug by her bed with a couple of other cat toys. She grabbed it, then sat back down and dangled it with her left hand so Mittens could play. That distracted the kitten so she wouldn't attack Taylor's ankle again while Taylor was writing down her ideas with her right hand.

At first she couldn't think of very many

good ideas to write down. She wrote *soccer* and then erased it.

"I'm definitely way better than any of those boys at soccer," she muttered, staring at the paper. "But they're probably better at it than my friends are. So our team might still lose."

She chewed on her lower lip. She could say the same thing about basketball, softball, running, and most other sports. For a second she wished her friends were as athletic as she was.

"Wait," she said out loud, sitting up straight. "That's it!"

She was so excited by her thought that she forgot to wiggle the shoelace for a second. Mittens let out a mew, which reminded her.

"Sorry, Mittens," Taylor said, wiggling the toy. "But I just had a great idea. I shouldn't only be thinking of stuff *I'm* good at. I need to think of some stuff that my *friends* are really good at too, and turn those into challenges. Ooh, I've got one!"

She wrote down *knot tying and untying contest*. That was something Emily and Jo were both really good at. They usually helped Taylor tie her shoelaces before her soccer games so they wouldn't come untied while she was running around out on the field. They also usually had to help her get the laces undone afterward. Both of them knew all kinds of knots. Jo's mother had taught her, and Emily had learned most of hers from books.

After that it got a lot easier to come up with ideas. Taylor just thought of stuff her friends could do well and then figured out challenges to go with those skills. For instance, Kara loved to eat. So Taylor decided they could have a banana-eating contest. She kept thinking of things she was good at too. For instance, even though her friends weren't that great at soccer, she figured if they made it a soccer goal-kicking contest instead of a whole game, they would still be able to beat the boys.

Soon she had a whole list of ideas. She read it over, trying to figure out what she would do to get ready in the morning before her friends arrived.

One thing was certain: This was going to be a different kind of sleepover than she'd originally planned. But she didn't mind. In fact, the change was sort of exciting.

"This is going to be so much fun," she whispered, picking up Mittens and giving her a hug. "It'll be like a sleepover with my best friends and a soccer game against my biggest rivals all rolled into one! What could be better than that?"

6

A Pair of Parties

"Where's Mittens?" Kara exclaimed as she bounced into Taylor's house the next day. "I've been dying to see her since I woke up this morning!"

Emily and Jo came in right behind her. Emily's dad had driven her to the sleepover and picked up the other two girls on the way. He was still on the front porch, chatting with Taylor's parents.

"There she is!" Emily cooed, pointing.

Mittens had just scampered from around the corner into the front hall. "Aw, she's even cuter than she was last time we were here!"

Jo giggled. "No way," she said. "That's impossible!" Taylor glanced toward the back of the house. She'd peeked out the back door just before her friends arrived. She hadn't seen the boys, but she'd heard them. It sounded like they were playing kickball or something.

"Come on, you guys," she said. "We can play with Mittens later. It's time for the sleepover challenge to begin!"

"Oh," Emily said, glancing at Jo and

Kara. "Um, are we really doing that?"

"Definitely! And listen, I came up with some awesome ideas for challenges that we can win. Like knot tying. Isn't that a cool idea? I'm sure the boys won't be expecting us to pick something like that." She grinned, still proud of herself for coming up with such interesting challenges. "I even got ready for it by cutting some long pieces of string and hanging them on wooden clothes hangers. We can hang the hangers on a tree branch so everyone can watch while each person does their knots."

"Knot tying?" Kara wrinkled her nose. "But, Taylor, you're always getting tangles just tying your shoes."

Taylor laughed. "I know. But I wanted to think of stuff we're all good at, not just me. And Emmers and Jo-Jo are great at tying knots, so they'll be able to win that challenge for our team. Right, guys?"

"Yeah, I guess so." Jo said.

Emily didn't answer. She was crouched down, tickling Mittens.

Taylor turned and headed for the back door. She could tell her friends were still a little distracted by the kitten. She didn't want to let them really start playing with Mittens or she might never get them outside.

"Let's go, team!" she called back over her shoulder. "It's time to show those boys who's boss!"

As soon as she stepped out into the backyard, she heard a shout. Max's head popped up over the hedge.

"Hey, you guys! They're here!" he called.

"What a surprise," Stan said, pushing his way through the hedge into Taylor's yard. "We were just about to give up and go inside. We thought you girls were too chicken to face us."

"Bawk! Bawk!" Randy followed Stan, flapping his arms like a chicken.

"Good one, Randy!" cried a fourth boy. He was a kid from the other third-grade class named Justin. Taylor didn't know him that well, but she knew he was on one of the other community soccer teams. He was a pretty good player. He and Max came through the hedge too.

Taylor put her hands on her hips. "Well, we're here now. So who gets to pick the first challenge? Should we flip a coin?"

"No, that's okay." Stan grinned at her. "You guys can go. Ladies first."

Randy hooted. "Yeah! Ladies first!"

"Let's pick that knot challenge you were just talking about, Taylor," Jo whispered. "Maybe if we can win something we're good at right away, the boys will get embarrassed and give up."

Emily nodded eagerly. "And then we can go back to our nice kitten sleepover," she whispered.

Taylor was so busy scowling at Stan and

Randy that she hardly heard them. "No way," she said. "We don't need any special treatment. You guys can choose first. We'll still beat you!"

Stan shrugged. "Fine, have it your way." He glanced at the other boys. "Come on, let's decide what to do first."

The four boys hurried off a few yards and huddled. Kara watched as they whispered and laughed. She looked anxious.

"Why didn't you pick first, like they said?" she complained. "Jo's right. That might have gotten us out of this stupid challenge thing sooner."

"It doesn't matter," Taylor said, staring at the boys. "We're going to beat them at everything anyway."

"Okay, we've got it!" Max announced, hurrying back over to the girls. "Our first challenge is . . . a water balloon fight!"

"Huh?" Jo said. "That's not a real sport. How do you even tell who wins?"

"Easy." Justin grinned. "Whoever stays dry the longest wins for their team."

"We'll be right back," Stan said. "The water balloons are all ready. We just have to get them from my house."

The four boys ran off. Kara let out a groan.

"A water balloon fight?" she cried. "Stupid boys! This totally stinks! I don't want to get my clothes all wet."

Taylor rolled her eyes and laughed. "Come on, Kara," she said. "I know you don't like getting messy. But it'll be worth it when we cream them."

"I don't know, Taylor," Jo said. "It's not really warm enough for water balloons, is it?"

Emily bit her lip. "I don't like getting stuff thrown at me," she said. "What if a balloon hits me in the face?"

"Step up, you guys," Taylor said, feeling a tiny flash of annoyance. She knew her friends weren't really that excited about the sleepover challenge so far. But she'd never expected them to be so wimpy about a few water balloons. "It's too late to back out now. Besides, we'll get revenge later with some of my challenge ideas."

Jo sighed. "Okay," she said. "I guess it'll be okay."

Kara and Emily still didn't look happy. But neither of them said anything. Kara just pursed her lips into a little O. Emily stared down at the ground and scuffed at the grass with her foot.

Just then the boys returned. Randy and Justin were each carrying a bucket, and Stan and Max were each carrying two. All the buckets were filled to the brim with water balloons.

"Here you go," Max said, dropping his two buckets by the girls. Stan put one of his buckets down too. "That's three buckets for you, and three for us."

"We'll set up over on that side of the yard," Stan added, pointing across the Kents' lawn. "You guys can stay here. When we're ready, we'll count to three."

"Got it," Taylor said. She picked up a water balloon. It felt slick, cold, and squishy in her hand. "Prepare to be soaked!"

"The only way we'll get soaked is if it starts to rain," Randy bragged. "Because there's no way a bunch of girls are going to get us!"

The other boys all laughed and high-fived one another. Then they ran over to their side of the yard with their buckets. All three of them picked up a balloon in each hand.

"Come on, girls," Taylor said, grabbing a second balloon herself. "Arm yourselves!"

Kara gingerly picked up a balloon. "Ew," she said. "It's all cold and slimy!"

"Ready?" Stan called over.

Emily and Jo each took a balloon out

of the bucket too. "Ready when you are!" Taylor called to the boys.

"On the count of three," Randy called. "One . . . two . . . three . . . let the soaking begin!"

He flung a water balloon at Taylor. She ducked, and the balloon burst against a tree. Then she let one of hers fly—straight at Max.

SPLASH! It landed right on his head and soaked him.

"Whoo-hoo!" Taylor crowed happily, already winding up to throw her second balloon. "That's what I'm talking about!"

7

Two out of Three

"Don't worry, Max!" Randy howled. "We'll get them back for that!"

Max pumped his fist. "Soak those girls!" he shouted as he sat down on the back porch.

"Don't worry," Stan yelled. "We'll get them!"

"Oh yeah? We'll see about that!" Taylor cried. She let her second balloon fly. It almost hit Stan, but he jumped aside just in time.

Taylor grabbed another balloon out of one of the buckets. As she straightened up, she saw Justin lob a balloon at Kara.

"Duck, K!" she shouted.

Kara squealed and jumped to one side. The balloon missed her and burst on the ground just behind her. Some of the water splattered the legs of her jeans.

"Aah, it's cold!" she cried, dancing around and shaking her legs. "Don't throw any more at me—I surrender!"

"What?" Taylor exclaimed. "Don't quit, Kara! You're doing great!"

But Kara didn't listen. She sat down in the grass.

Taylor frowned. She couldn't believe Kara was just giving up like that. But she forgot about that when she saw a water balloon spinning toward her out of the corner of her eye. She had to fling herself to the ground to avoid being hit.

Whoa—close one, she thought as she

leaped to her feet again. *Stay focused, Kent.
You can still win this.*

She looked around to see how the others
were doing. At that moment Stan tossed a
balloon at Emily. She tried to jump out of
the way, but she wasn't fast enough. The
balloon burst on her shoulder and soaked
her shirt and the bottom part of her hair.

"You're out!" Randy yelled, pointing at her. "That's two down and two to go!"

Randy was so busy dancing around and laughing that he wasn't paying attention to anything else. Taylor hurled her balloon at him. It hit him square on the chest.

"Hey!" he yelped in surprise.

Taylor laughed. "Two down and two to go," she taunted. "Let's see if I can make it three down!"

She grabbed another balloon and threw it at Stan. But he dodged it easily.

Meanwhile, Justin had just grabbed two balloons. He let one fly at Jo. She jumped back, and it burst at her feet. Before she could react, he flung the other one at her. This time it hit her on the leg.

"You're out, Sanchez!" Max called from the porch.

"It's okay, Jo-Jo," Taylor called. "You did great!"

For the next minute or two it was Taylor

against Stan and Justin. Finally she managed to hit Justin on the ear with one of her balloons. That left just her and Stan.

"Ready to give up like your friend Carrotina did, Taylor?" Stan taunted, tossing a water balloon from one hand to the other.

"Not on your life." Taylor scowled at him.

"Get her, dude!" Randy shouted from his spot on the porch. "Show her how stupid she was to think a girl could beat us!"

Stan grinned. "Yeah. *If* she's really a girl."

Taylor could tell he was trying to make her mad so she'd mess up. But she wasn't going to fall for that. She aimed and threw, but the water balloon missed its mark. A second later Stan threw one back at her. That one missed too.

"Go, Taylor!" Kara cheered. "You can do it!"

For the next few minutes Taylor and Stan battled against each other. They threw tons of balloons, but they all missed. Soon the buckets were almost empty.

"Looks like it's going to be a tie," Jo commented.

Taylor frowned. She didn't want a tie. She wanted to win!

She reached for another balloon. Stan had just grabbed one from his bucket too.

"Get ready to get wet," Taylor said, taking aim.

Just then Stan looked off toward the house. "Hey, Taylor," he said, pointing. "Isn't that your kitten? What's she doing outside?"

Taylor gasped. Had Mittens escaped from the house?

She whirled to look where Stan had pointed. There was no sign of Mittens.

"Look out, T!" Kara shrieked.

But it was too late. A second later Taylor felt something smack her on the side of the head. Cold water soaked her short, curly hair and ran down her neck.

She couldn't believe it. Stan had conned her! "That was a dirty trick!" Kara exclaimed.

But it was no use. The other three boys were already rushing to high-five and congratulate Stan.

"We won! We won!" Randy howled at the top of his lungs.

The other girls wandered over to Taylor. "Never mind," Emily said. "You were really good, Taylor. If he hadn't tricked you, you probably would have won."

Before Taylor could answer, the boys came strutting toward them. "Ready to give up and admit boys are better than girls?" Max asked with a grin.

"Not a chance. It's our turn to pick the

next challenge, right?" Taylor said. "Well, we pick knot tying."

"Huh?" Justin blinked. "Knot tying isn't a challenge."

"Yeah." Randy laughed loudly. "It's what most of us learned back in kindergarten!"

But the girls insisted. "It's our choice, right?" Kara said.

Stan shrugged. "Whatever," he said. "You'll lose this one just like you lost the first one."

"We'll see about that," Taylor said. She ran inside to get the hangers and string she'd prepared.

Soon the two teams were busy tying and untying each other's knots. And just as she'd hoped, Jo and Emily were the only ones who could get all the knots untied!

"Way to go, Emmers and Jo-Jo!" Taylor cried, running over and hugging them both at the same time.

Jo laughed and hugged her back. "Thanks. That was actually kind of fun."

"Uh-huh." Emily smiled and pushed back her hair, which was still wet from the water balloon. "Plus, it gave us extra practice tying your soccer shoes."

"Whoo-hoo!" Kara cheered. "Girls are the champions!"

Taylor laughed, happy to see that her friends finally seemed to be getting into the spirit of the challenge. "Totally," she said. "We should probably get double points for that one, since you both won."

"Forget it." Stan looked annoyed. He had been worse at the knots than anyone else. "One point per challenge, that's the rules. So we're tied. One win each."

"Yeah. And it's our turn to pick next." Randy folded his arms over his chest and smirked. "And we pick . . . bug collecting."

"What?" Taylor's heart sank. "What do you mean, bug collecting?"

"Get the jars, guys," Stan said. As Max ran off toward Stan's house, Stan grinned at the girls. "Each of us gets a jar. Whoever has the most bugs in their jar after fifteen minutes wins."

Taylor shuddered. There wasn't much that scared her. But creepy-crawly insects and spiders had always made her nervous. She wasn't scared to be outside with them flying around or underfoot, but she hated the idea of touching them or having them crawl on her. Her friends had helped her mostly get over that fear one time when they were camping out in Emily's yard. Still, Taylor definitely wasn't looking forward to picking up insects and spiders and carrying them around in a jar.

She could tell that Kara wasn't exactly thrilled about the idea either. "You mean we have to pick them up with our fingers?" she asked.

Stan shrugged. "You can pick them up with your toes for all I care," he said. "They just have to end up in your jar." He turned and stared at Taylor. "I hope you *girls* aren't too scared to handle it."

Taylor scowled at him, furious. She was sure one of the other boys had told him about her fear. That was why they'd picked this challenge. They hoped she wouldn't be able to compete.

But she wasn't about to give them the satisfaction of seeing her quit. Max was already returning with a box full of glass jars. Taylor grabbed one of them.

"Okay, let's go," she said, unscrewing the lid from her jar.

"Are you sure?" Stan was still grinning.

"I'm sure."

Justin checked his watch and counted down. As soon as he said "Go," Taylor dropped to her knees. There were always lots of bugs around in the springtime. She was sure she could collect more than anybody else if she just ignored her nervousness and did her best.

It wasn't long before she spotted a centipede wriggling through the grass. The first time she tried to pick it up, she almost dropped it. But then she pictured Stan's face sneering at her. That would be a lot ickier than touching a few bugs. She dropped the centipede into her jar and started looking for more.

By the end of the fifteen minutes, she had a lot of creepy-crawlies in her jar: beetles, spiders, worms, several centipedes, and even a moth. She hoped when they counted them up, it would be enough to win.

It turned out to be *almost* enough. She came in second in the count, right behind the challenge winner . . . Emily!

"Way to go, Emmers!" Taylor exclaimed. She should have known her friend would be great at that kind of challenge. She loved all animals, even bugs. Whenever she saw a fly in the house, she always wanted to shoo it out a door or window instead of squishing it.

"There," Emily said, opening the top of her jar and releasing her bugs back into the grass. "That's best two out of three, right? Now can we quit?"

"No way," Randy said immediately. "Not unless you're scared to face us in a *real* challenge."

Stan pointed to the net set up in the yard. "Yeah. How about a game of badminton? You said you could beat us yesterday, right? So let's do it. Unless that was all just a bunch of girly talk, of course."

"Come on, you guys," Kara complained. "Do we really . . ."

"You're on!" Taylor interrupted, glaring at the boys. "Badminton it is. Get ready to lose!"

8

More Challenges

For the next couple of hours, the sleep-over challenge raged on. The badminton game was close, and Jo played especially well, winning most of the girls' points. But in the end, the boys won by two points.

Next was the soccer-goal challenge. Taylor set up her practice net at the far end of the yard and brought out her ball. "Whoever gets the most points in five rounds wins for her team," she announced, dribbling the ball expertly.

"Don't you mean wins for *his* team?" Max said.

Taylor shrugged. "We'll see about that," she said. "Pick your goalie, you guys. I'll shoot first."

The boys were all pretty good at soccer. But Taylor was a good goalie and blocked a lot of their shots. Even though the other girls didn't do too well against the boys' goalie, Justin, Taylor made every one of her shots. That meant the girls' team won the challenge.

After that the boys picked the beanbag toss. They'd seen the wastebaskets Taylor and Kara had set up the day before, and they were sure they could beat the girls at their own game. According to the boys' new rules, there wasn't just one winner — the whole team's points got added up together. There were four rounds. Taylor scored on four out of four of her tosses, but Emily and Jo only got two points each and Kara didn't manage to score at all. Meanwhile, all the boys got at least three points, so their team won.

The boys also won the banana-eating contest that the girls chose next, much to Taylor's disappointment. She was pretty sure that Kara hadn't tried hard enough to win that one. But she didn't say anything about that.

The boys' next choice was a sack race. Max and Taylor were neck and neck until Max tripped over a root and fell down. After that, Taylor won easily.

It was the girls' turn to pick again, and they chose croquet. The boys made fun of the choice, laughing and calling croquet a sissy sport. But they weren't laughing anymore when Jo beat everyone else and Taylor came in second.

"We're ahead by one win again," Jo said

as the girls returned their croquet mallets to the holder. "Isn't that enough? Can we stop now?"

"Not yet." Taylor glanced over at the boys. They were huddled nearby, probably trying to figure out what challenge to choose next. "I don't just want to beat them. Not after all the obnoxious things they said. I want to trounce them!"

"What's that mean?" Kara asked.

"'Trounce them' means pretty much the same as 'beat them,' only a little stronger," Emily explained. "Like, if you win a soccer game by one point, you beat the other team. If you win by ten points, you trounce them." She knew a lot of words from reading so many books.

"Maybe we should pick a vocabulary challenge next, Emmers," Taylor joked. "You'd trounce everyone at that one!"

Jo sighed. "It's almost dinnertime, and we still haven't had a chance to play with

Mittens," she complained. "Why are we wasting our time with a bunch of boys?"

"We still haven't made cookies yet either," Emily reminded them.

"Yeah," Kara grumbled, licking her lips. She loved Emily's father's cookies. "I thought this was supposed to be a fun sleepover, not gym class. Or a day with my stupid brothers."

Taylor shrugged, glancing over at the boys again. They were still whispering together. She wondered what they were talking about.

"We can play with Mittens and decorate cookies when it's too dark to play outside," she promised her friends. "Right now we have a sleepover challenge to win. And I have an idea for the next challenge."

Kara groaned. "I hope it's a cookie-making challenge," she mumbled. "I still need to get the banana taste out of my mouth."

Taylor didn't pay any attention. She called the boys over.

"Okay, the next challenge is a good one," she announced. "Dodgeball!"

"What?" Emily squeaked, looking alarmed. "Um, Taylor . . ."

"Dodgeball it is!" Randy said right away, sounding delighted. The other boys looked pleased too.

"We can use Taylor's soccer ball," Stan said, running over and grabbing it from where it was sitting in the grass near the goal. "This is going to be awesome!"

"Yeah," Justin added with a laugh. "You girls are going down!"

"We'll give you a few minutes to tie some pillows and stuff around you for armor if you want," Max offered with a smirk.

"We won't be needing any pillows," Taylor said, grabbing the ball out of Stan's hands. "But you guys might want to grab some tissues, because we're going to make you cry like little babies."

"Oh yeah?" Randy retorted. "Well, I—"

"Taylor!" Gloria called, interrupting him. The housekeeper had just stepped out on the back porch. "There you are."

"Hi, Gloria," Taylor said. "Check it out—we're a point ahead! We won the soccer contest, and also the—"

"Never mind that," Gloria interrupted again. Taylor noticed that she looked worried. "Did you girls bring Mittens outside to play?"

"Huh? No, of course not," Taylor said. "We've been busy with the sleepover challenge. Isn't she inside with you?"

Gloria shook her head, looking more worried than ever. "I can't find her anywhere in the house," she said. "Taylor, your kitten seems to be missing!"

9

Lost and Found

Taylor gasped. Then she whirled to face the boys. "Did you have something to do with this?" she cried. "If you jerks took my kitten, you'd better give her back right now!"

But the boys looked either worried or confused. "We didn't take your kitten, Taylor," Max said. "We swear."

"Yeah," Stan added. "Why would we do something like that? Anyway, we've been out here with you the whole time, remember?"

Taylor still felt a little suspicious. But Emily tugged at her arm. "I'm sure they didn't do it," she said. "They're kind of obnoxious, but they're not that mean."

"You kids have been running in and out a lot this afternoon," Gloria said, glancing around the yard. "Mittens might have dashed out without you noticing when you opened the door."

Taylor bit her lip. Gloria was right. The girls had run in and out of the house several times. Taylor had gone in to get the rope for the knot tying, the beanbags for the toss, and the bananas for the eating contest. And Emily and Kara had each gone in once to use the bathroom.

"Oh my gosh," she muttered, picturing Mittens wandering around outside all by herself. What if the noise of the competition had scared her and she'd run away?

What if she ran all the way around the house and out to the street? "Mittens!" she called out, feeling frantic. "Mittens, where are you? Here, kitty kitty!"

"Here, Mittens!" Randy joined in, looking anxious. "Yo, cat, where did you go?"

"Maybe it's hiding in the hedge," Justin suggested.

"We have to find her!" Emily had tears in her eyes. "She's too little to be outside all alone!"

"Hold it!" Stan exclaimed. "Don't panic, you guys. We'll never find that kitten if we just run around yelling and stuff. Let's stop and think for a second."

Jo nodded, stepping forward. "Stan's right," she said in her calm, logical way. "I'm sure Mittens couldn't have gone far. If we're organized about this, I'm sure we'll be able to find her quickly. Why don't we split into teams?"

"Good idea." Stan nodded. "One team can search the backyard, one can check the yards next door . . ."

"And two more can search inside," Jo finished. "One upstairs and one downstairs. That means we need four teams total, so we'll have two people on each team."

Taylor took a deep breath. She was still anxious and scared, but now she felt a little bit more hopeful. If anyone could figure out how to find Mittens, it was Jo!

"Okay," Stan said. "Kara, how about if you and Randy search the yard here. I'll check my yard and the one on the other side. Who wants to come with me?"

"I'll do it," Justin offered.

"Good," Jo said. "The rest of us can look inside. Taylor, why don't you and Max search downstairs and Em and I will go upstairs."

"Sounds like a good plan, kids," Gloria said. "While you're doing that, I'll check the basement again. Taylor's parents already looked in the front yard."

Soon Taylor was searching the first floor of her house. She left Max looking into all the kitchen cabinets while she headed out to check the other rooms. She found her father in the front sitting room. He was on his hands and knees, peering under the sofa.

"Have you found her yet?" he asked, sitting up.

Taylor shook her head. "I hope she's not

really lost," she said, her voice shaking. "I should have been watching her better."

"Never mind," her father said. "Just find her first, and then you can worry about blaming yourself if you want, okay?"

Taylor nodded, knowing he was right. She kept searching, checking the fireplace in the sitting room, the TV cabinet in the den, and even behind the toilet in the powder room. But there was no sign of the kitten anywhere.

She stopped in the powder room doorway, trying to be as logical as Jo and figure out where she hadn't looked yet.

Maybe Gloria's right and she slipped outside when the door was open, she thought. *I wasn't paying that much attention when I came in to get those beanbags out of the back closet. . . .*

"That's it!" she blurted out, suddenly realizing one place where she hadn't searched.

She rushed to the laundry room at the rear of the house. There was a closet near the back door where the family kept their casual coats and outdoor clothing, as well as some of Taylor's sports equipment and other backyard games. Flinging open the door, she immediately laughed out loud with relief. There, curled up in a big basket of gloves and scarves, was Mittens!

"I found her!" she yelled to the others. Then she scooped up the kitten.

Mittens opened her eyes and yawned, her tiny pink tongue curling out of her mouth. Taylor nuzzled her soft fur with her chin.

"I'm sorry, Mittens," she murmured, smiling as the kitten's whiskers tickled her face. "I must have been so distracted by the competition that I didn't see you go in here when I opened the door to get the beanbags."

The kitten started to purr. She didn't seem to mind at all that she'd been stuck in the closet for an hour or so.

Kara rushed in and skidded to a stop in the laundry room. "Did you say you found her?" she asked breathlessly. Her eyes widened as she spotted Mittens in Taylor's arms. "Whew!" she exclaimed. "There you are, Mittens!"

A second later Emily and Jo arrived too. The boys were right behind them. They were all relieved to see the kitten safe and sound.

"Thanks for helping me look for her," Taylor said to the boys.

Max shrugged. "No problem."

"Yeah. I'm glad you found her. She's cute." Justin reached over and tickled Mittens under the chin.

Taylor turned to her friends. "I just realized I've been totally crazed over this whole sleepover challenge," she told them. "I'm really sorry. I shouldn't have made you guys do it when you didn't want to."

Jo sighed and smiled. "Good," she said. "Does that mean we can end these stupid challenges and go back to having fun?"

"Hold on!" Max protested. "I'm glad you found your kitten and all. But the sleepover challenge isn't over!"

"That's right," Randy said. "We need a chance to catch up."

Stan nodded. "You're only one win ahead, and we definitely would have thrashed you at dodgeball."

Kara squeezed her eyes shut and groaned. "Oh no!" she cried. "Here we go again!"

Taylor looked at her. Then she glanced at Jo and Emily. They both looked worried. She guessed they were thinking she wouldn't be able to resist the boys' challenge. In fact, it was awfully tempting to take it up, especially since she was awesome at dodgeball. . . .

But she shook her head and smiled. "You're right," she said to Max. "You guys probably would've won at dodgeball. So why don't we just say you get that point and call it a tie?"

"A tie?" Stan sounded dubious.

But then Justin punched him on the shoulder. "Come on, that's good enough," he said. "If we're done with this girl stuff, we can go in and watch the monster movie we rented or play that new video game you were telling us about."

Stan's face brightened. "Cool," he said. "Okay, it's a tie. But we'll win for sure next time!"

"Next time?" Kara squeaked.

Taylor grinned at the look of horror on her face. "Don't worry, K," she said. "I learned my lesson. I know you guys don't like sports and contests and that kind of stuff as much as I do. And sleepovers are supposed to be fun for *all* of us—not just me."

Emily looked happier than she had all day. "Does that mean it's time to play with Mittens and decorate cookies?"

Kara nodded. "And play dress-up!" she cried.

"Sounds like fun," Jo agreed with a smile.

Taylor glanced at the boys. "You can stay for a while if you want," she offered. "There are plenty of cookies to decorate."

Kara giggled. "And dress-up clothes to wear," she added.

"Ew!" Randy shouted. "No way, José!"

"Yeah. Come on, guys, let's go watch that monster movie," Stan said. "We can make popcorn to go with it. That's way better than some stupid girly cookies."

"Yeah!" Justin cheered, trading a high five with Max. Then they all ran off, out of the house.

Jo laughed. "Okay, maybe those boys aren't quite as obnoxious as we always thought," she said. "But they're definitely still boys!"

"True," Emily agreed with a giggle.

"Yeah, but they're gone now," Kara said. "So let's get started with our sleepover."

Taylor grinned. Competing against the boys had been fun. But nothing was more fun than hanging out with her three best friends.

"You're on!" she said.

Slumber Party Project:
Friendly Competition

It's possible to have fun competing at sports and games without turning it into a war like Taylor and Stan did. Why not have a sleepover challenge of your own at your next party? You can figure out the games and activities ahead of time or come up with them together once your friends arrive. You can pass out ribbons or other awards to the winners of each contest, or let the person who wins the most points choose what kind of pizza to order or what to watch on TV, or anything else you like. Just remember, the prize shouldn't be as important as having fun! If you like, you could even vote for

which player showed the best sportsman-
ship and give that person a prize too!

Here is one idea for a fun contest to get
you started:

BEANBAG TOSS: Set up clean wastebaskets,
buckets, or any other type of sturdy container in the backyard or in your room.
Assign a point value to each container. The
closest ones could be one or two points,
and the ones that are farther away or have
smaller openings could be three or five
points. You can use beanbags or any other
small, soft item to throw—even rolled-up
socks will work! Give each person a certain
number of tosses, and add up the total number of points to decide the winner.

Now go ahead and think of more activities
of your own. Have fun, play your best—
and always try to be a good sport!